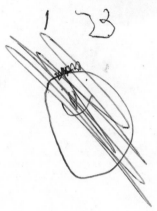

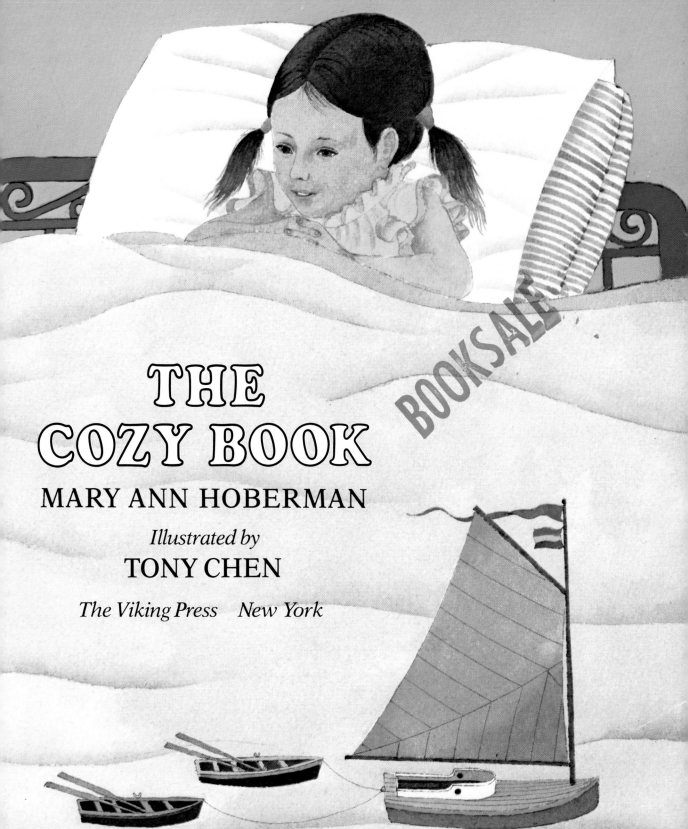

THE COZY BOOK

MARY ANN HOBERMAN

Illustrated by
TONY CHEN

The Viking Press   New York

For Denny and David

First Edition. Text Copyright © 1982 by Mary Ann Hoberman. Illustrations Copyright © 1982 by Tony Chen. All rights reserved. First published in 1982 by The Viking Press, 625 Madison Avenue, New York, New York 10022. Published simultaneously in Canada by Penguin Books Canada Limited. Printed in U.S.A.
Library of Congress Cataloging in Publication Data. Hoberman, Mary Ann. The cozy book. Summary: Verses relate a variety of things perceived as being cozy. 1. Children's poetry, America. [1. American poetry] I. Tony Chen. II. Title. PS3558.03367C6 811'.54 80-10916 ISBN 0-670-24447-3 AACR1
1 2 3 4 5 86 85 84 83 82

When you wake up bright and early
In your roasty toasty bed
With your covers wrapped around you
And your pillow on your head
And you peek out at the morning
That's a cozy kind of way
To begin the cozy doings
Of a very cozy day

You get up a little later
And you put some cozy clothes on—
Shirt and sweater, corduroys—
And after you have those on
It is time to eat your breakfast
So you sit down in your seat—
Later on come lunch and supper—
All the cozy things to eat!

Scrambled eggs stirred soft and sunny
Melted cheese that's nice and runny
Fresh-baked muffins dripping honey
Chocolate pudding, bread and butter
Fluffy mounds of mashed potatoes
Jelly doughnuts, milk and cookies
Toast and tea when you are sick
Applesauce strained smooth and thick
(Lumpy food is never cozy)

Juicy peaches fat and fuzzy
Sliced bananas, tapioca—
Sliced bananas? Tapioca?
Well, certain people think they're cozy
You may not
Some don't
Some do

What you like is up to you
(But everyone thinks cocoa's cozy)
Whipped-up frothy orange Jell-O
Chicken soup with spots of yellow
Creamed tomato red and rosy
Cozy cozy cozy cozy

Afterwards you go and play
What are cozy things to do?
Pat-a-cake and one potato
Piggyback and peekaboo

Cozy games that last all morning
House and store and school and doctor
Setting up your tracks and trains
Getting out your boats and planes
Making roads for cars and trucks
Building towns with blocks and bricks

If it's nice, you go outside—
Sandbox, seesaw, swing and slide—
All the cozy games to play
Which ones will you choose today?

Flying kites and jumping rope
Tag and hopscotch, hide-and-seek
Bouncing balls and blowing bubbles
Blindman's buff (but do not peek!)
Dig a hole straight down to China
Build a castle in the sand

Hide inside a weeping willow
Plant a garden
Start a stand
Make believe and let's pretend
Tell a secret to a friend
Sing a-ring-around-the-rosy
Cozy cozy cozy cozy

Sniff the air for cozy smells
Smell of flowers, fire, food
Roses blooming
Wood that's burning
Bread that's baking
They smell good!

Fresh-dug earth
New-mown hay
New-cut grass
New-born day
Washing drying on the line
That smells fine!

Popcorn that has just been popped
Kitchen floor that's just been mopped
Onions that have just been chopped
Stop your crying!
Smell them frying!

Some smells make you think of things
Things you think you had forgot
If a smell helps you remember
Call it a forget-me-not

Places that you like smell cozy
People that you love smell cozy
You do, too
To you, you do!
(How to tell a smell is cozy?
You won't know unless you're nosy!)

Cock your ear for cozy sounds

Bird cheep

Mouse peep

Bug buzz

Brook burble

Bee bumble

Baby babble

Lip smacking
Toe tapping
Cheek popping
Hand clapping

Tongue clicking
Clock ticking
Wood chopping
Wave lapping

Straw sipping
Rain dripping
Fan whirring
Cat purring

Chick cluck
Duck quack
Goose honk
Pig oink

Sheep baah
Horse neigh
Cow moo
Cock crow

Mud squish
Snowcrust crunch
Snap of dry leaf underfoot
The gurgle that a gargle makes
The giggle when a tickle takes

Hurdy-gurdy
Music box
Bells that jingle ting-a-ling
Piano tinkle
Pipe of flute

A little strum upon a string
A little tune you like to hum
A little song you like to sing
A little whistle on your lips
Music is a cozy thing

Traffic rumble
Airplane roar
Freight train toot
Grandpa's snore
All sound cozy
From afar

Laughs and chuckles

Squeaky kisses

Whispers, murmurs, lullabies

Hush and listen!

Close your eyes!

What sounds cozy through and through?

Say it softly—

I love you

Words are cozy

Mumble
Scribble
Sandal
Muzzle

Alabama

Cuspidor and Orphan Annie

Pachysandra
Sarsaparilla
Tusk and smug and fog
Galoshes

Ambidextrous
Henrietta

Amble

Wobble

Dawdle

Mosey

Listen

Cousin

(Close to cozy)

Superstition

Baked Alaska

Dandelions

Hummingbirds

Busybody

Dillydally

Ali Baba

Cozy words

Cozy places?

Attics, cellars

Closets, cupboards

Nooks and crannies

Halfway up or down the stair

Underneath a chair or table

Tucked behind a screen or curtain

Cozy places?
Alleys, tunnels
Caves and secret passages
Tent and treehouse
Clubhouse, haystack
Hideaway in rocky hollow
Places that are hushed and hidden
Spaces that are dark and warm

Go and find your teddy bear
Snuggle underneath your blanket
Cover up from top to toesy
Cozy cozy cozy cozy

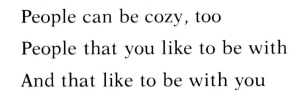

People can be cozy, too
People that you like to be with
And that like to be with you

People who can understand you
People who will hear your troubles
People who will keep your secrets

People who have pleasant voices
People who have happy smiles
People who know how to listen
Like to play, tell jokes and stories
Like to help you, like to *like* you
Like to laugh but not at you

Sometimes they are skinny thinny
Sometimes they are roly-poly
Sometimes short and sometimes tall
Sometimes young and sometimes old
Sometimes he and sometimes she
But whatever they may be

They are always nice to be with
Nice to stay with
Spend the day with

Laps to sit in, hands to hold
Arms to hug you when you're cold
Lips to kiss you, soft and rosy
Cozy cozy cozy cozy

Cozy feelings deep inside you
Gay and happy
Snug and warm
Slow and steady
Mild and peaceful
Nice and easy
Safe from harm

Calm

Unhurried

Smooth

Unworried

Fine and dandy

Tried and true

Lovey-dovey

Hunky-dory

Cozy feelings

Felt by you

Other kinds of cozy feelings
Things to feel that feel so nice
Petting puppies
Patting mudpies
Finger painting
Sucking ice

Lick a lolly

Blow a candle

Pick a posy

Hold a hand

Catch a snowflake on your tongue

Scrunch your toe into the sand

Whittle down a stick of softwood
Kick a pebble on a path
Squish into a squashy cushion
Sink into a brimming bath
Back rubs, bear hugs, cuddles, squeezes
Sneezing long-awaited sneezes
Laughing till you're all in stitches
Scratching in the place it itches
Whiskers (when they're not too prickly)
Tickles (when they're not too tickly)

Gliding in a squeaky glider
Rocking in a rocking chair
Swaying in a swaying hammock
Cozy feelings everywhere

Cozy things we haven't named yet?

Turkey stuffing

Rabbit tail

Turtle

Thimble

Birthday presents

English sheepdogs

Ginger ale

Lucky pennies

Circus ponies

Macaroni

Curly hair

Cradles

Dimples

Apple dumplings

Cotton candy

Solitaire

Hot fudge sundaes

No-school Mondays

Picture postcards

Matching twins

Unbaked batter

Butter fingers

Monkey business

Safety pins

Four-leaf clover

Yankee Doodle

Jack-o'-lantern

Sugarplum

Chocolate kisses

Spring vacation

Hibernation

Bubble gum

Shiny lockets

Zipper pockets

Easter bunny

Honeycomb

Wells for wishing
Going fishing
Going barefoot
Going home

And now the cozy day is gone
And now the cozy book is read
Of all the cozy things there are
The coziest of all is bed
So go to sleep, sweet sleepyhead
Just curl up snug and shut the light
A goodnight hug, a kiss goodnight

Sweet thoughts
Sweet dreams
Sleep deep
Sleep tight

Droopy
Drifty
Drowsy
Dozy
Dream of everything that's cozy